NOT BY WORDS ALONE

Ray Wade

River Push Books
Columbia, South Carolina

ISBN-13:978-0692279281
ISBN-10:0692279288

For information about bringing Ray Wade to your live event for an interview, reading or book talk, contact Ray at crwade@mindspring.com.

Produced in the United States of America

River Push Books

549 Sulgrave Drive

Columbia, SC 29210

www.RiverPushBooks.com

Thank you to members of The Twisted Scribes Writers Group for encouraging me to keep writing and who challenged me to write better, edit endlessly and pursue to publication. Fran Rizer, and I are the surviving members and I especially appreciate her unfailing friendship and teachings on the craft and business of writing well.

Gaynell Gavin, author, neighbor and friend has inspired me to continue with this project.

Thank you, Pamela Jolley, for sharing your sweet spirit with me and for bringing this volume to print.

Some of the pieces included here have been published previously. Special appreciation to:

> The Free Times Colossal Short Story Contest, 1999 e-published *Fred.*

> The "Not Yet Dead" Poets Society 1997 Chapbook included *Louise.*

> Ellen Waterston and The Fish Trap Writers Conference selected *Falling in Flower* for the 2012 Fish Trap Writers' Conference Zumwalt Prairie Outpost Anthology.

DEDICATION

This publication is dedicated to my dear friend and writer, lover of all things musical, feeder of birds, seeker after mature faith, who cared for dogs and worked tirelessly for peace in this world, the late R. Leonard Jolley.

CONTENTS

INTRODUCTION

These original compositions are to be read aloud in an oral performance. Written over a period of thirty years, the writings reflect the author's deep emotional response to experiences with the outside world. The title reflects a sincere belief that writing and printing of words alone is insufficient to communicate the essence of life's transforming experiences.

POEMS

How does a poem mean?

John Ciardi

MARIPOSA

I found a lily where one ought not be.

Growing out of volcano rubble in a dry swale.

Snow last tended it and all the others alongside.

From a distance I thought snow lingered on the black rocks

High on the prairie

Beneath the July sun.

I hiked closer.

Saw the likes of a flight of butterflies feeding on flower stems.

I arrived and found flower petals shaped like butterflies

Colored as white with pale pink and blue at the base

Where the body would have been.

I pressed the butterfly like flower feeding there

And brought the white and pale colored wings for you to see.

I should not

But just one would not matter I thought.

But matter it did.

Later I **would** know.

I held it in my hand.

Quiet and soft

It rode my pocket.

A delicate burden of care.

I happily brought it over hours of walking

Then we met at the pasture gate.

I ran and hugged you.

I squeezed the petals in that display of love.

Leaving a little, sticky, fragrant spot.

I showed the treasure.

Only my scented palm.

All this for you.

FALLING IN FLOWER

Awake at Coyote-O-Five

I rolled out of my tent

And

Fell into you-

You-You-funny little bunch faced flower.

As I thought to rise and apologize

You grabbed hold and touched me

With a sigh.

What could a man do?

But dig in and hang on?

Had I mistaken my new love's intent?

No-

She kept holding me tight.

Want to know a secret?

I liked it.

She smelled so good!

I mean, really wow!

Like straw, honey, dirt...

Not exactly dry nor wet,

Cause if she smelled like wet dirt

>That could mean mud and oh, well,

>Mud doesn't smell good.

While I wondered out loud how to describe her

She, little miss flower face,

Squeezed me and said

"Shh, Let me sleep."

"OK" I said

"But how long before I can wake you?"

"Just wait. I will tell you."

You, possibly, by this time, are thinking

There is nothing serious here and ordinarily,

I'd agree but not this time.

Our random experience was extraordinary

>To The Infinity.

It was neither about living nor dying

>Much more important than that.

It was Flower Power Love

I'm talking about how it feels to

      Hold and be held at the same time

To be one with another when the other wants

To be one with you.

"I want to sleep some more," she said.

I closed my eyes and told brain and body to be quiet

      and still.

Foolish attempt to comply with my own self when that self

      was ready to

Rip and roar, take off on a run with my flower love.

Then,

To my thrill she turned to face me...

Pretty eyes with petal lashes blinking

Slowly, seductively.

"What does this mean?" I asked.

"It means we, you, are going to be quiet and listen."

I moved closer.

She blinked s-lo-ow-ly and smiled.

"What do we listen for?"

"Shhh!"

Next came a sound

The whispered unfolding of

A butterfly wing in the breeze.

"What was that?" I asked.

That, sweet one...

Is the new soft sound of you.

Newly awakening you.

A poem after reading Joseph Campbell

Tat tuam asi

Thou Art That

True Believer

True to what Belief?

Be yourself

Be your own person

Be what you is fo if you be what you aint
You aint what you is

There you are

You be there

That is you

Thou art that

Tat tuam asi

You are.

I am.

God is not fact. Eternity is neither future nor past, but now.

Joseph Campbell

LOUISE SAYS SOME SONGS

Louise is my very good friend who loves beautiful music and can make up words to music she hears. She will not attempt to sing, and since she can neither read nor write, she asks me to write down what she says. She calls them "saysongs." They have power to change things in her life.

The poet is anti-specialist.

Saturday Review of Literature, early 1960's.

SUITE OF YOUR ARM (title is my own creation)

Sweet is your arm when it wraps around my shoulder

God gave it to you for your girl

Just to hold her.

Your arms are just your arms while they hang by your side.

Come and loop them around me and

We'll walk together the whole world wide.

Sweet is your arm when it wraps around my shoulder

God gave it to you for your girl

Just to hold her.

An arm's just an arm

Until you do something with it

And reach out to use it

To connect you and me.

Sweet is your arm when it wraps around my shoulder

God gave it to you for your girl

Just to hold her.

Louise credits this saysong with bringing her husband back the
only time they had been separated in 23 years of marriage.

It takes life to love life.

Spoon River Anthology, Edgar Lee Masters.

THAT'S THE WAY

I turn to the left

I turn to the right

But I'm all alone in the middle of the night.

I think of the things that we used to share...

But there's only one thing honey,

Do you still care?

Is this the way you want it?

You over there without me?

As long as you're gone

That's the way it will be.

Well, I'm begging for mercy

Please come back to me soon

I don't like it none

Alone in this room.

Is this the way you want it?

You over there without me?

As long as you're gone

That's the way it will be.

As long as you live like somebody else says,

You're not thinking your heart through;

Your life's just on the edge.

Plunge in now deeper,

In my tear-stained eyes.

Come back to me darling before the sunrise.

I can't change things baby

I can't turn back the clocks

I can only clean up the bedroom...

Pick up yore socks

My love for you darling

Will not fade away

Come on home darling, come back today.

Is this the way you want it?

You over there without me?

As long as you're gone

That's the way it will be.

SON OF A WHIRLWIND

Pretty much due North of Saddle Butte in the Zumwalt

East of Troutshoe, T Pasture-Coyote and Hay Meadow

Surrounded on the North by Pine Creek Bench

South by Saddle Butte and East by Dan Goertzen Homestead

If I'm ever lost and you want to find me

Check out Wade Place

It's on the map

Over there on the table

Held in place by two boards so the mice

And winds do not take it away.

Wade Place...waiting to be discovered

By this son of an ancient Creek girl, Whirlwind,

The barter bride who seized her chance

When the West was East

and swirled her age with the English man in need of care...

Mixed his mind with her blood

Then whirling, dancing, bounced their seed

Up and Over the Great River TomBigBeeee

On the stream called Sunflower

Swirling up not so much a storm as

A steady turning form where we now call Alabama

Fanning over the earth and

Skipped and hopped her way across Texas

To Taos to the Pacific then

North to Whistler and turned back toward where she'd come.

Blessing the earth with her dance of life

Leaving us all behind,

She turned out her spinning, thinning

Great Spirit

One with Him

She whirled away

Leaving me here.

SKETCHES

You don't talk to Louise so much as you experience her.

LOUISE TALKIN' AT ME

The store Louise thought she bought sits on the riverbank above Little Hell Landing on the Savannah River, facing west. The harsh sunlight burns my face on a hot afternoon. I hold a photo of the clapboard building, highlighted by the rusted tin roof that shades the porch. Advertisements for Goody's Powders, Union Oil, Ice, Coke, Grocery, Bait 'N Tackle show up clearly. Customers rest on the worn benches between the white and blue ice freezer and the faded red kerosene pump. Brown and curled leaves of the sycamore trees hang down in front. A familiar sign we need rain.

My nostrils tickle, a familiar response to the dust of the road. I hear the branches of the sycamores scrape across the tin roof and metal signs over the storefront. The ice freezer hums. I remember the smell of coal oil, the locals' name for kerosene. The arthritis twinges in my right elbow as I remember turning the crank that raises kerosene to customers' containers.

A good photo invites you to look more than once, lets you see into the shadows. This one turns on my imagination. Not only can I see into the shadows, I see inside the store, through the screens and behind the closed wooden doors, and back in time.

My friend Louise sits beside the ice cream box and prays for all the children of the world. Rev. Gary, self-appointed pastor of Little Hell, fusses over the foolishness of some Holier Than Thou. Friends are nearby, getting along as best they can. Heaven and earth may be soothing, peaceful and cool somewhere but not here. A low burn from the sand of the road heats my shoes and irritates the soles of my feet. I want a cool heavenly breeze to blow over and wrap around me. Not quite ten in the morning. And already the shade gives no cool, nothing more than a silhouette. The heat mirages distort my vision. Rising vapors from decayed leaves bring a muddy smell. My brows knit from stuffiness and headache, the everyday touch of hell that reminds me I am alive.

This store and a few houses on the bank of the river make up as much as there has ever been of this town. Not much of one, but a real place named Little Hell in the state of South Carolina. You will not find it on a map and likely would never hear of it if not for this story.

Around here, summer starts in April and lasts until November, sometimes even into December. A long time ago the riverboat captains gave this place its name because they had to make a series of complicated maneuvers to get into the landing. Most boats had to back out in the river one or more times to navigate the sharp turn and avoid big rocks to get in here. Now the only things left are the river landing and the name they gave it -- Little Hell.

This place makes people over. The folks here have changed me some, too. Louise first, then the others turned my name around and changed my life. They call me Preacher Paul. I am not a preacher though I am the son of a Preacher.

I live on the edges of light, in the early morning and late evening shades and shadows of the Savannah River. I am a photographer. I capture slices of light in a camera then squeeze those tracks into ink and onto paper.

People from somewhere else often assume we need help or that we need to be saved. We're OK, here on our side of the river. We're first to see the light of a new day and first to see the dark every evening. Not many babies are born here, and the few who are grow up and leave pretty soon.

I arrived a few years after my birth and stayed because of the river, the people and the store. Guessed I would always stay around these parts. Now most of the folks are gone, the store is closed, shelves empty, advertising signs gone. I am still here and my camera continues snapping shots where I point it. Click!

Little Hell is my home. I dearly love the people, the land, water, plants, animals and even the bugs. I only wish it were cooler. And I wish it would rain.

**

The store's tin roof snaps, creaks and pops as the sun edges out of the shadows and heats the day. The heavenly cool breeze did not come. It was all in my hoping anyway. September in the South Carolina lowcountry feels like left-over summertime. Mid-day light is harsh, lousy for photos. That part of each day I walk over to the store.

What we had was a day too hot for the birds to sing. When I pushed open the door a horrible moan set up. "OOOOh!" It sounded again. "OOOOh." The retired Rev. Gary O. Davis sleeps every night under the counter of the store. He stays here as watchman, a favor to the owner, Louise Broome, who recently became concerned about terrorists. Louise came in through the back door just as I entered the front.

"Lordy, Lordy, I tol' him. All that moaning will do is to make people think he's drunk. Preacher Paul, I told him."

I looked over behind the counter. The noise came from Rev. Gary for sure. A fly flap hung on a cup hook behind the counter. I picked it up and gave a good loud Whop! on the counter right above his head. "OH HELL!" he moaned.

Louise and I moved at the same time, the floorboards squeaked with our steps. We met at the ice cream box where she put down her armload, pulled up a chair, and settled in. We say her day's work consists of guarding the ice cream box.

A few years back, Louise came into some money and bought the store when the prior owner, Holiness preacher Sister Dolly got sent up the river for running drugs and not paying taxes. Louise had a vision, said the Lord had called her to save the store and lead the people back to God. Her vision and spunk sustained her. Unable to read, hard of hearing, and generally called a re-tard by those who do not know her, Louise is a very good friend to most every person who lives in and around Little Hell.

And from the windy west came two-gunned Gabriel.

Dylan Thomas

GARY O - A STORY

When we were preacher boys at Howard College, all of us on the football team used the streets of downtown Birmingham to cruise for babes. None of us had a car so we'd thumb a ride into town and go prowling on foot.

One day we saw a person, possible female, about half a block ahead and walking away from us. As we got closer, there were many clues that she may be unattractive in the extreme. Gary was first to react, grabbing at his heart, staggering and feigning an attack of nausea.

Her hair was thin, greasy and stringy. She wore a World War II A.L.I.C.E.(Alice) pack, cut off jeans, too big around the waist, and big socks that rumpled down her painfully thin legs and sagged around her ankles, just below numerous briar scratches, cuts, and bruises. This female person had broad shoulders and bony arms with pointed elbows covered in ragged, scabby skin.

We walked fast and caught up with her at the next corner. Before we had seen her face, Gary told us he would brave the dangers and speak to her. Then he pulled us together in a huddle and said, "Get ready boys, this will likely require protective eyewear." Then, having no idea of her name and wanting her to turn so each could see her at the same time, Gary hailed her with; "Hey, Joe!"

As expected, she turned to us and that almost prompted a laugh in itself. But we stood quiet as we checked her face up and down, back again. She had thick eyebrows, crooked teeth, a pointed chin with a double mole and three hairs. Her very long nose had a horizontal dimple on the end and acne covering most of it. If she knew herself to be ugly, it did not show as she replied, "My name is Jessica." To which Gary replied, "I'm a bible major and my initials are G.O.D. Please call me Gary."

He then turned to us and said in a hushed tone, "Get right and get quiet for we are all in the presence of holiness. I've never seen a kinder face."

TATTOO

Tattoos and the people who have them attract my interest and draw out my imagination. I cannot remember a time when I did not want one on my body. Mobile, Alabama, where I lived the first years of my life in the 1950's, is a seaport. The men in our family who were not sailors or seamen had once been and every one of them had the tattoos to prove it. The number of times they had shipped out could be estimated from the number of tattoos they had. A real mystique surrounded where they were when each tattoo was applied. Personal history could be easily extracted if a kid asked, "Where'd you get that tattoo?"

There were so many different ones, regular jail or brig types adorned fingers, New Year's eve in Singapore accounted for daggers through skulls, a trip to South America yielded a black panther walking down a limb, Hawaii or the Philippines usually resulted in a woman in a grass skirt or nothing at all that could dance seductively when biceps were pumped.

Mom was quick to advise me these were forbidden things, of course, a transgression against the Lord, desecrating the holy temple of the human body. When she told me this, I always wished I had been born to my aunts and uncles to thereby be relieved of the burden of being Raised Right. Baptist church attendance didn't help either. I figured one day in the future I'd grow up to be big, strong, and mean like my cousins. Then I would break free of fundamentalist convention and parental expectations and Get A Tattoo.

It didn't happen. When I turned thirteen I was still planning but I couldn't decide what kind of tattoo I wanted. No one would let a thirteen year old son of the local deputy sheriff into a tattoo parlor anyway. I'd decide by the time I was sixteen and joined the navy. When I came home for shore leave at the end of my first tour, I would have the problem solved.

It didn't work out that way. I stayed in high school, went to college, married, and went to work. Every now and then I'd see some Harley Davidson wings on a bicep, "Mom" or a heart with a girl's name and set off thinking again. I always knew I'd get my tattoo when the time was right but when would the time be right?

A few years ago, I began noticing old and aging women with blue barbed wire bracelets tattooed to the sagging skin of their ankles or wrists. Occasionally, I'd glimpse a flower or braided rope on shoulders or a bare midriff of women almost as old as me who had undoubtedly enjoyed the free lifestyles of the sixties. Then I began to notice a new popularity of tattoos among young men and women...my time had come! Now people my age were getting ears pierced and tattoos that they had longed for.

"You'll have to live with it the rest of your life...you'll be sorry." Again I had been warned, and once again I could not find the right time for my tattoo. I still haven't settled on a design. I have some time left to decide and to do it when I am good and ready. I thought that at fifty-five years old I'd be much better equipped to make these life-long decisions. Now, I find myself thinking maybe by sixty, even seventy-five.

Having felt with fingers that the sky is blue,
What do we have left to look forward to?

Louise MacNiece

WILD WINGS

The mid-day is dark with storm clouds, wind gusts and intermittent rain when I meet with other state agency representatives in a newly constructed state office building.   Large windows give me an excellent view of the outside while we discuss some mind-numbing topic pertaining to our mutual efforts for the state. I look through the open door when I hear the whistle of wood ducks and the sound of wings. In the corridor, a pair of wood ducks settle into a pool. It is a pool of light cast on the floor by the overhead fixtures. The drake leads the hen to check out the middle, then round the edges of the pool. Dissatisfied, perhaps, they clatter up, bank sharply, and fly out of sight around the corner. Gone!

Other witnesses speculate. Someone says the birds had to come in through the loading dock. I think it is more likely they used a service hatch. Another worker doubts they came in through the reception area since no one called security. What is our policy on ducks inside state facilities? What harm could they do?

The next morning my office is a mess. Pictures are broken, but only the ones with water in the scene. Feathers are all over everything, the floor, desk, papers, books, bookcases, and chairs. The ducks had roosted in my silk flower arrangement next to the aquarium. I tried to imagine them, faced in opposite directions, huddled together on a branch of driftwood. Curious, I track them to the atrium water-garden. Sunlight sparkles on droplets from the fountain.

I watch a peaceful scene as each one follows the other around, round, and around again. They dabble, then preen and shake glistening feathers. I am glad they have come.

I wonder why they chose this place. There are more suitable places for ducks than this artificial nesting and imitation wetland of fountain and water garden. I well understand the biologists when they describe loss of natural habitat as a major cause of reduced numbers of ducks and changes in their migration patterns. Before building here, men cut down trees where wood ducks roosted. We directed water from the surface into underground culverts and catch basins. French drains move water quickly away from the building to prevent ponding and foundation decay, and deny breeding habitat to mosquitoes.

Before this building was here, we had trees and grasses and water in pools, streams and, waterfalls. We got rid of all that. Then we styled the inside like the outside used to be. We did not plan for ducks. Now ducks spoil the plans we made for ourselves. Those of us who like things the way they used to be can travel far away to places protected and preserved.

My thoughts take flight. Are we experiencing the first of an evolution or is this the onset of a fowl revolution? It could be we now face a new breed of aggressive Wood Duck. There may be others to come. Hundreds of thousands, flocks of every kind of duck, goose, willet and snipe. Will a new breed of swooping swans come after us through the automatic doors, threatening every Lida lady of our kind? Where will we hide from geese coming to goose us? What shall become of us?

Questions directed to me by the group leader break my terrors, bring me back to conference room three forty-seven. After a moment of work my attention again lags. I am listening for the sound of wings.

The novel is a prose narrative of some length that has something wrong with it.

Randall Jarrell

SHORT STORIES

FRED[1]

Fred is standing by-side the road staring at a telephone pole. For two hours now he has wondered over a sign tacked to the pole. "Phil's Place." Wonder which Phil that is, the psychologist feller up at state hospital when Louise went crazy or the one what's a preacher over at the Muleyville Church? There were two other lines on the sign, "Crickets and Beer, Bread and Worms." *They sure ain't got much,* Fred thought.

Fred does pretty much what he's always done which is work different days for different folks. Cash only. He works one day each for four different fellers, they each pay him at the end of the day. Fred figures he has a four-day workweek and every day is payday.

For two weeks, Fred's been trying to get over Louise being gone. She's gone, and that makes him walk a lot, sleep very little and feel tough-like, hard on the outside but soft, like as to soak up water, on the inside. Fred figures that's why he can't cry.

---

[1] "Fred" was published online as honorable mention in the Free Times Colossal Short Story Contest.

Two, that's his lucky number. When he left home he had two shirts. He met Louise two years later. When Phil, the psychologist, asked him about Louise, Fred said he'd known her about two years, but that was all he knew about her. Then she got well after two more years in the hospital.

As Fred goes through his day at each job, he keeps track of what Louise would be doing if she were at the trailer or over in her room. Now she's talking to the kitchen table, then talking to people who come by for one of them songs she makes up for them. Right now she's staying with Fred's Aunt Mae at one of them senior centers. Fred never could help his Aunt Mae, so he is thankful for Louise to return all the favors Aunt Mae had done for them all these years.

The day before Louise left, Fred came to the house, went straight to the bedroom and put all her things in two clean, stout paper grocery bags. When Louise came home, he was sitting in his chair on the porch by the front door, them bags beside of his foot, staring straight ahead. The TV was on inside, and the news man was talking about the big fire over at James' trailer sales place and Sister Dollie's Tabernacle. They's talking about something strange causing the fire and about investigating what all had been going on there.

"What's they all talking about?" Louise asked.

"Whatever it is, it ain't good," Fred answered.

That's how it was between him and Louise. She was always talking and could hear real good. Fred hadn't heard a word since he got sick when he was three, didn't talk much and listened real good. Louise could hear but never listened. She asked lots of questions. Fred could answer anything that ever bothered her. Some people called it lip reading, but Fred called it paying attention to Louise. Sometimes Louise didn't even know she was bothered and Fred already knew the answer. He felt real well-off when he thought about it.

"We need to start walking," Fred told Louise. They picked up the bags. Fred knew a way through the saw mill he worked ever Thursday. That put them on the highway to Hattiesburg in less than fifteen minutes. They walked all night.

The sun was just starting to pink-up the sky when they knocked at the center where Aunt Mae was staying. When the door opened, Fred surprised the lady inside. He handed her both bags of Louise's things and said, "This here's my wife's stuff and her, she's my wife." Nodding his head in Louise's general direction he told the lady, "I'm leaving her to help with my Aunt Mae." Glancing at Louise, he squinted his eyes to keep from crying and walked back home.

They'd met each other at a church homecoming. Both were from the same neck of the woods, but Louise had been away at that hospital since she was a little girl. Two years later they were married. His lucky number again.

Fred missed Louise. Her voice all warm, the smell of her hair and neck next to him at night, that clear sweet-toned voice. Louise always has kept herself pretty. Always combed back the long hair she never cut once since she started going to the Holy Ghost Tabernacle and playing the tambourine.

This evening after he cleaned the trailer and before going to bed, Fred spent some time in thought. Sitting as it did, at the end of a long road to the top of a clay gulley, the trailer was in a good place for thinking and watching the sun go down. No one ever caused any trouble out here, even when he walked down by the highway like right now. Fred could think here. He liked to think about things slow and easy and from both sides, like breathing in and out.

He and Louise had done everything they had ever tried. They lived together ever night of their 12 year marriage until tonight. And they never let down anybody who counted on them.

They went to Florida once with some church people. But Fred didn't like the way they did things. He was about church like some men were about getting married, he'd tried it twice but it never took neither time.

That didn't stop Louise none. She kept going and praying and singing, then she came home saying she'd been preaching and making up them songs to give to people when Sister Dollie preached.

When she told him about all the money people gave at the Tabernacle, Fred knew something wasn't right. He'd been raised up with those folks and if they had any bunches of money, they'd keep it for themselves. He knew that for a fact.

Louise didn't care about that. She walked around inside that trailer talking about all the wonderful things the Lord was doing and how she was the Lord's handmaiden. If Sister Dollie was willing to give her a place to minister, Louise was going to take it.

If Louise ever found that Sister Dollie or James were doing wrong, what would she say to them? "Tell it. Tell it and confess your sin." Louise would do anything, anything except give up on God. "No, no, no," she practices. "You can beat me, you can kill me...Go ahead and kill me but you and me we all know that God don't love ugly. No, No, No!"

Fred just went on living like he always lived. He never worked more than four days a week and never spent more money than he had.

A silent warm strength took over Louise. It showed itself in her keeping on preaching and doing songs at the Tabernacle.

James would read the Bible to her every day so she would have something to preach about. James had given her a special room in one of the trailers he had for sale. Folks could go there and she'd give them a song. They'd write them on the walls, the ones that could write. It was pretty.

She would be back at home with Fred ever night. Louise expected Fred to complain about what she did ever day. But he never did. She believed he'd understand about the Tabernacle people. He believed she would see the light. Neither of them ever did.

It was the night before the Tabernacle's second birthday service and Fred thought they'd been mighty lucky not to get caught doing whatever it was they were doing wrong. Food was ordered for the people to eat after service. Louise had brought home the new dress Sister Dollie gave her to wear to services Sunday. Now Louise was getting her things laid out for the morning.

"It ain't none of it right," Fred said. They had been silent about it for almost two years now. "It ain't you what's doing nothing wrong, Louise, it's all them others. There's too much money, too many hands and too little work going on. God just ain't in it."

Louise laid her fresh Kleenex down. "I trust the Lord's judgment. He knows the hearts of men and women, too."

"Does he ever say anything about it, though?" Fred asked.

"If he does, I'll never hear him, we both know that," answered Louise.

Fred looked surprised, then said, "I love you, I rilly, rilly love you. I do."

"Then how you gonna show me?" Louise asked.

Their loving went smoothly. It always had. Whatever they did was agreed to. Fred adored Louise. He'd protect her with his life. She wanted to give him the same affection and comfort.

Fred finally learned the truth the day before Louise went to help Aunt Mae. His boss at the fish camp told him the law was looking into James' trailer sales business and the folks at the Holy Ghost Tabernacle. They're cooking up drugs in Louise's room in that trailer and then sell them and put on a show with the offering at the Tabernacle. Make it look like all those poor people suddenly have lots of money and are giving it all to God.

Fred had come straight home and packed up her things. When he got back from walking to Hattiesburg, it wasn't more than a couple of hours before Sister Dollie and a bunch of them from the Tabernacle came around. "Is Louise here? Oh please tell us she is," they'd all said.

"Well, she ain't." Fred told them. They all took on a crying and carrying on awful like.

"There was a trailer fire and by the time they got it put out there was this body where somebody died in it. We just knew it was Louise but we hoped not." Sister Dollie told Fred. "We'll miss her, such a loss, oh, we needed her so...now don't you go doubting God's ways, Fred. You just trust in Him 'til you see her again one day."

Fred said, "Yes Ma'am."

They all got in their car and were almost to the highway when the sheriff come and arrested them all. After they were all gone to jail, Fred walked out to the road to watch the two police cars drive away.

At seven-thirty Fred is still out by the highway. His boot sole makes a scrubbing sound as he shuffles his right foot, first left, then right, then back again. The wind is rattling the black jack oaks sprouted around the light pole. In two weeks he will go visit Louise and Aunt Mae. Aunt Mae will smile at him and Louise will talk at him.

"You love me, you really love me." Fred will tell Louise. He knows because she went to help Aunt Mae just because he said she needed Louise to help her.

Louise was a saint, Fred figured. It was a secret most folks would never know because they didn't listen to Louise like

Fred did. He thought maybe someday other folks would notice all the good possibilities of Louise. She made most folks kind of uncomfortable. Louise did not know how to lie, and some thought that would be the end of her, what with her not listening too. Fred thought those folks were always wanting too much from life.

He turned from the highway and headed back towards the trailer. He rubbed his hand over the top of his head. He would adjust his cap if he wore one, but Fred never wore a cap. Just before entering the trailer he stopped, stretched tall, and opened his arms wide, like when he hugs Louise.

TURRIBLE TURRIBLE

You could have blowed me over with a feather. My Fred, my own dear sweet husband Fred, said for me to leave. He come in from work at the sawmill just about like most other days.

What it was that set me off to notice something different was him carrying some brown paper bags folded up under his arm. All he did was say I was to leave and just as soon as we got me packed. Then he went to pulling out all my clothes, my medicine and anything I didn't always carry in my purse. He must of thought I had a lots because he brought four of those sacks like they put your groceries in when you buy them over at the IGA store. Well, least wise, like they used to do back before they went to using these little bitty plastic ones they's got now. We never needed but one and a half of them big old brown paper sacks to hold everything and we's ready to go.

Set in to walking and, boys, now I'm here to tell you we *walked*. All night long we walked. The sky was just pinky sort of when Fred left me off at the nursing home where his aunt lived. Have you ever walked all night long, without stopping nor nothing? Well me neither, never before. But I done it then, and when we came up to the back kitchen door of that place, Fred, he told the lady in charge there I'd come to help out with his aunt and he'd be back to get me when it was safe for me to be to home. He kind of blinked back a tear when she took my bags and said it would be okay for me to stay.

That lady that runs the place is some of Fred's kin, too, so she didn't have to ask all them questions about phone number and all. She already knowed we don't have no phone.

I thought it was something turrible turrible at the time but it turned out it wasn't. It was a gift from God.

That was the night the Hallelujah Tabernacle and Hotel burned up with somebody in it. The next morning, Sister Dolly and all them that worked for her got arrested and I came into all that money so's I could buy my store.

FRIENDS

You could say we never understood nothing. But how could we have known the life other people learned? Just as we got started living, we'd been taken for a ride of an afternoon, just after Christmas for me, and never brought back. They drove us off to a place we'd never seen and left us there at what they called a school. There wasn't no classes at first, just a bunch of other children.

All of them was the same, almost, as me. Unable to tell what or why, when they turned us out in the playground we gathered up together. Laid down in the dirt, made a little pile. There we held to each other and, since we didn't know what else to do, cried. Let me tell you it was one big sad sound out there in God's sunshine.

Somebody finally turned our whimpers into a word. We said it together, right after, only louder cause it was all of us. Too, we'd had some little time to think when we said it, so's our word was full of remembering.

Even if we learn slow and forget fast, some of our remember works like most folks. After all these years, I remember how those other little girl bodies felt cold, sticky, and warm, at the same time. We breathed our bad breaths together for they wouldn't let us have no toothbrush of our own for fear we'd hurt ourselves or one another with it. Some of us were better off than others, but they treated us all like we was the worst off of the bunch. There in that little lump we smelled like pee.

Then that little girl said another word we hadn't thought of and we said it too, together. Like a bunch of monkey babies chattering boo hoo and a big boo hoo. Then we said our words together.

"Ma-Ma."

"Gohome."

***

Fred said if it was him, he'd just go home, that's what Fred said. I told him he was always smarter than me and I had no notion of which way to go, that's what I told him. "Good Grease! What do you expect anyhow?" I said to him. That's what I said.

Besides, that's where I learned how to pick out a good friend. Fred better be glad because that's how I knew he would be my husband. See here now, the ones that make good friends are the ones you can do the most for.

I was telling Fred the other night that I can't handle more than two good friends, him and Rev. Gary. Fred don't really understand about being friends. I told him he's my husband and that makes him my best friend and he better not forget it. Then I told him Rev. Gary is my friend too, just as good as he is.

Well, he said it didn't make no sense to him neither ways. Then he said it didn't make him no never mind but Rev. Gary better not try to be nothing but a friend. That's what Fred said.

I said, "Fred, what you mean? He's a preacher, the one that married us." I kind of yelled it, might have hurt Fred's feelings but not so I could notice.

Fred, he said he remembered what I said about how I liked the way Rev. Gary looked better than I liked Fred's looks. Right off, I remembered when I said it. Rev. Gary come up to the house wearing one of them nasty old mustaches. I told Fred that if I could, I would tell Rev. Gary's wife that if she knew what I knew, she'd make him shave it off. Fred asked me what I knew about Rev. Gary that Rev. Gary's wife didn't know and I said I knew how good he looked without that mustache, that's what I told Fred I'd tell her. Would if I could.

I think Fred may be jealous. Wonder if anybody else thinks he's jealous. I do, I think Fred's jealous. That's not a bad thing. I don't think it's a bad thing for Fred to be jealous. Just a little bit.

Lordy! If it's bad for Fred, him being jealous and all, I think I better quit being a friend to Rev. Gary. I don't want to do that though. That preacher brought me through too much. Oh, but I don't want to hurt Fred though. Rev. Gary was the first one for me to tell I was gonna get me a man and love him, love him, love him. And I shore did and I shore do. Ever time I think about how much I love Fred I just want to go a hollering. Whoop! Whoop! Whoop!

Fred's awful good to me. He works so hard and him so dumb, too. Oh, I don't mean dumb in a bad way. I just mean, like, when I get my hair done and I'm settin' here and he comes home. He don't say nothing and I say, 'Fred, look at my hair, you better look at my hair! I done gone all the way over there to that beauty parlor and spent your money. You better look at how I got my hair done up pretty."

He'll look around, and I'll ask him how he likes it and he'll say it's all right. That's just the sweetest thing when he says that. I can always tell he really likes it when he says that and it makes me love him so. I get all jittery inside and my heart goes about to burst. If he didn't like it, he'd just say "hunh," but I don't know what I'd do if he ever did. He never has. Ever time he's said that same little thing, that soft and bashful sort of, "It's all right," it gives me the goose flesh all the way down to my toe nails.

***

Course I know this place he's got us to live in is a mess. Looks like we're junkyard bound. Fred's always saying if I can do better then go ahead on. But this place, it ain't really bad, and it is all ours. When Fred's mamma and daddy died and left it to him, he wanted to sell it. But I said we needed a place to live and why not live here, and Fred said, "Don't make me no never mind."

It weren't three days before he put up a sign, storm blowed it down last spring. It stayed a long time though. Big old thing, heap of people must have seen it. Big black letters on a white piece of plyboard. I can't read but he told me it said Fred's Fill Dirt. When he put it up there, I said it wouldn't do no good. No phone, no address. He said, "They all know. They'll come up here to the house."

I told him, "Shoot. That sign'll do as much good as those men they put up there on the moon with people starving and having wars and stuff here on the earth." He didn't say nothing. The next thing you know, ever day or two somebody'd buy some of that dirt his mamma and daddy left for him. Been about nine years now, and Fred says if they keep buying his land at this rate, we can sell it and live on it, too.

They's bought and hauled off most everything except the drive from the mailbox to the trailer house, both sides and all around back. I said to him, "Yeah and Mr. Smarty, what you gonna do if they buy it all up and leave us setting here in this trailer on a mole hill in a hole?"

Well, he just told me he'd let 'em pay us to dump stuff here. Said it's the latest thing in trash. Called it a landfill. I just wish people who think Fred ain't smart would have heard what he said next. Fred said the very same ones what paid to haul this place away will pay again to bring it back. Now ain't that wonderful?

I am so blessed to have a man like Fred for me to love. I'm so proud of him.

We can do just about anything we want to. We can. It's the power of two.

Gary O's translation of one bible verse stuck in my
mind. Jesus said to his disciples,
"Make those children come here to me."

One of the proofs of immortality of the soul is that myriads have believed it – they also believed the world was flat.

Mark Twain

CHILD'S PLAY: A SERMON
ONE BIG THING IN FIVE STANZAS

Let's pretend we are in charge of the world and everyone is playing with us. Pretend everybody does exactly like we ask them to do because they love us and we love them.

I

This world needs our devotion to what makes us all better people.

Were I to make my list of what is required, it would not include:

A long range strategic plan with goals, objectives and Action Steps

A political Action Committee

A Bill for Congress

A President

No. We must take a look at fractals, those tiny discoveries by physicists that attempt to explain why we can't quite get to any fixed point, the need of a gyroscope's wobbly precision in space travel, and why the coast of Britain looks straight and solid as we reenter from space, only to watch it curve various ways as we get closer and appear solid as a rock until we land on the beach with a mouthful of sand (no two grains alike).

Fractals push away from each other but have hooks to keep them connected. This explains, some say, how our world holds together and accounts for different forms of beings. I also believe it explains something inherent in ourselves, this top predator, that causes us to pack up our own, stake our claim, cut one or more out of the herd, cut down the only tree around, build an earthship and live in it, find rivers to be dammed and un-dam them, fashion a factory, make money and move away from others taking ninety-nine percent from the one percent without a care in this world.

II

I struggle
Toward the sunrise
Wanting more
        of
What today will bring.

Today,
A perfect day
To think of a pig
My mystical walking pig
Free from the hog wire I found.
Sunrise and a runner
Runs

Up the hill

Into the light

Gathering promises for today.

I open my eyes

To pray

To see

   or

Maybe only to glimpse

The One Who Comes.

III

Now I give to you what was given to me.

Words help us to think to do the best, be the best.

Sit, listen to the silence and hear...

"Someday, after we have mastered

   the winds and the waves

   the tides and gravity

We will harness for God the energies of love,

     And then, for the second time

     In the history of the world

Man will have discovered fire." Teilhard de Chardin (of the Garden)

IV

Sit and See what comes to us.

V

Now UP! We sing and dance! Joyous children of Glory...

It's OK

> And now we can

It's OK

> And now we can

It's OK

> And now we can

IT'S OK AND NOW WE CAN!

YEAAAAA!!!!!! CLAPPPP!!!!!!!

Bio

Ray Wade has studied the Arts, Sciences and Humanities since age nine when he read all the volumes of a Book of Knowledge Encyclopedia during summer break from Whistler Elementary School near Mobile, Alabama. His professional career in pastoral ministries, private non-profit community service organizations, and South Carolina State Disabilities agencies spanned more than forty years.

Now retired, he enjoys hunting, photography, and volunteer activities in environmental conservation. He and his wife Carol live in Columbia, SC, with their magnificent Maltese named Razz.

www.ingramcontent.com/pod-product-compliance
Lightning Source LLC
Chambersburg PA
CBHW070648130626
46555CB00006B/2766